Text © Writers Four Rise and Shine Dancing Pencils Writing Club
2004
Cover Design © Patricia Devenish 2004
Photographs © Felicity Keats 2004

First Edition

No part of this publication
may be reproduced, stored in a
retrieval system, or transmitted in any for
or by any means, including photocopying, without written permission
of the publishers

umSinsi Press
PO Box 28129
Malvern
4055
Kwa-Zulu Natal
South Africa

web: http://www.umsinsi.com

ISBN 1-86900-525-2

# THE PEN TELLS IT ALL

Anthology of Stories and Articles

By
Four Rise and Shine
Dancing Pencils Writing Club

# CONTENTS

| Title | Author | Page |
|---|---|---|
| Prologue | Phasekile Radebe | 6 |
| Foreword | Felicity Keats | 7 |
| Author Biographies | The Authors | 8 |
| H.I.V./AIDS Counselling | Phasekile Radebe | 9 |
| Alcoholism | Phasekile Radebe | 15 |
| Know Your Frame of Mind | Phasekile Radebe | 21 |
| The Song of Parental Love | Phasekile Radebe | 25 |
| As Tough As a Woman | Gloria Gladys Khanyile | 29 |
| The Pre-Democratic Life in A Township | Barbara Gumede | 33 |
| The Beautiful Valley Where I Grew up | Gloria Gladys Khanyile | 36 |
| On Her Majesty's Coronation | Gloria Gladys Khanyile | 41 |
| Wounded Spirit | Barbara Gumede | 44 |
| Good Neighbours | Gloria Gladys Khanyile | 50 |
| The Misfortune of Tsepo | Barbara Gumede | 52 |
| The Thief | Barbara Gumede | 55 |
| Men and Mourning | Phasekile Radebe | 58 |
| Do I Know my African Culture, Norms and Values? | Phasekile Radebe | 61 |
| You are Now a Man, my Son | Barbara Gumede | 63 |
| Ukwemula | Gloria Gladys Khanyile | 65 |
| The Process of a Zulu Marriage | Victoria Ngane Cele | 69 |

# PROLOGUE

The presentation of miscellaneous stories by "Club Four Rise and Shine" provide you (the reader) with a warm feeling and enjoyment in reading without contemplating on one perspective.

Information written here displays a background of African tradition, culture, norms and values, history, geographical and social aspects of South Africa, adventure, health education and experiences. It also provides the reader with skills in child-rearing and personality moulding, as well as leisure reading material.

This book is a collective effort to avail valuable information for reference by our future generations, as most information is based on originality of cultures and norms of our African people, most of which is still practically adhered to nowadays.

We owe our gratitude to Mrs Felicity Keats for her encouragement and support in our efforts, enthusiasm and zeal in book writing.

**Writers:**
Phasekile Radebe
Gloria Gladys Khanyile
Barbara Jabulile Gumede
Victoria Ngane Cele

All nurse-pensioners of Umlazi, KZN.

# FOREWORD

At the start of 2003, four retired nurses from Umlazi, near Durban, visited me. They had a fervent desire to leave their footsteps behind for the benefit of others.

They wanted to write a children's book, but after having a right brain freewriting lesson from me, the work that they produced was so interesting that I suggested that they rather wrote some stories from their life experiences.

They were very happy when they left my home. Nine months later I heard from them again. They wanted to visit me. They arrived on appointment at 1.00 pm and only left at 5.30 pm ... in the time they were here they read to me an entire book they had written.

As we were beginning with writing clubs, they chose their own name: Four Rise and Shine Club. They are so enjoying what they are doing, that may train as mentors and run writing clubs of their own ... What a benefit for society.

Here follows the book they wrote between them which has been typed and minimally edited. Their footprints are here for those who follow! To know who these four wonderful women are, here follow short author biographies written by the authors themselves.

Felicity Keats                          July 2004

# AUTHOR BIOGRAPHIES

**Phasekile Radebe (nee Mkhwandazi)**
Was born at Inanda, just outside Durban, educated at Inanda and trained as a nurse at McCord Hospital. Worked at different hospitals within KZN. Got married in 1980. Unfortunately was not blessed with children. Her hobbies were dancing and reading.

**Gloria Gladys Khanyile**
Born at Mariannhill near Pinetown. Educated at Pinetown Primary School and at Mariannhill St Antony School and St Francis College. Trained as a professional nurse at King Edward V111 hospital. Married and blessed with one son, Nkosiyezwe. Taught at the King Edward V111 Nursing College until retirement.

**Barbara Gumede**
I, Barbara Gumede, (born Mangole) attended school at Inanda Seminary. After completion, I went to King Edward VIII hospital to train as a nurse. I qualified, thereafter married a Mr Gumede and had four children and have now seven grandchildren. Two of my children are married and the other two are not married. I am now retired and stay in a township house.

**Victoria Ngane Cele**
Victoria Ngane Cele nee Makhathini was born on the $22^{nd}$ January 1938 at a rural area of Ntshongweni situated thirty-five miles away from Durban. She was educated at St Albini Catholic School. After completion, she went to King Edward V111 hospital, Congella, Durban for training in General Nursing and Midwifery. In 1972 she went to Baragwanath Hospital for a Diploma in Orthopaedic nursing science.

She got married in 1960 and was blessed with five children; four sons and one daughter. All are married. She has fourteen grandchildren. She is now retired.

# H.I.V./Aids Counselling

By Phasekile Radebe

A young man called Yebo-Yebo (*Yes-Yes*) lived in a rural area, very far from town. His parents worked in Johannesburg, and only came home twice a year, and they would bring him nice clothes from the city.

This made him very popular amongst the young ladies of his age group. He would boast to his friends of having more girlfriends than any boy around.

Yebo-Yebo got ill with many bouts of flu and his uncle took him to a popular *inyanga* (witch-doctor) who told him that he was bewitched by other young men because he took their girlfriends. The witch-doctor started treating him, but he did not improve. He gradually lost weight, had prolonged fever, persistent coughs, recurrent sores in the mouth and had a sore throat, and generalised swelling of the lymph glands, especially the neck glands, and eventually had diarrhoea on and off, within short intervals.

Yebo-Yebo returned to his witch-doctor to report that he was not responding to treatment. His witch-doctor told him that he was going to give him stronger medicine, but he needed to pay him five hundred rand immediately. The young man did not have that money, so he wrote his mother in Johannesburg, who came immediately. She was surprised to find her son in such an ill condition. She took him to the hospital where he was investigated, blood was taken for analysis, and was found to be HIV Positive.

He was by now very weak and malnourished. The doctor admitted him to hospital against his will, but his mother encouraged him to accept admission for better care, so he did. His doctor also explained to him that if he was not well cared for nutritionally, his HIV would soon complicate into AIDS.

Yebo-Yebo did not know much about HIV/AIDS. In

fact, he was one of those young men in denial that HIV/AIDS was such a serious incurable disease, and did not even believe in safe sex.

An AIDS Counsellor visited Yebo-Yebo the following day to counsel him. She introduced herself, and then asked him if he knew why he was hospitalised.

"I have been bewitched, Nurse, but the doctor says that I am HIV positive, and if I am not well cared for, I will complicate to AIDS," announced Yebo-Yebo carelessly. "So what is this HIV/AIDS?" he continued.

"I am glad that you want to know, Yebo-Yebo," responded the Counsellor. "Now let us talk. HIV is a virus or germ that gets into the body of a human being, and reduces the body soldiers that protect us from disease. Aids is a chronic illness which impairs the body's ability to fight infection, with the result that the body becomes susceptible to life-threatening diseases." The Counsellor then continued breaking down her explanation into simpler language for Yebo-Yebo to understand.

A – Acquired > the virus infects the person.
I – Immune > the soldiers of the body become
   affected and fail to defend the body against
   infection.
D – Deficiency > the virus weakens the soldiers of
   the body.
S – Syndrome > the collection of different signs
   and symptoms occurring from the disease,
   sickening the person.

"Sister, I am told many people in South Africa suffer from this disease. If that is true, how do they get it?" asked Yebo-Yebo.

"In many ways," responded the Counsellor. "Sexual intercourse, through infected semen and vaginal secretions, is a common way of transmission. An infected mother infecting her unborn child is another way, as they share the same blood. Through syringes and needles that have been contaminated by infected blood. Blood transfusions with infected blood and blood products. Contact with contaminated blood or wound secretions where the skin is broken, as in lacerations and cuts. A child can also get it from the breast milk of an infected mother.

"When the virus enters the body, it attacks the body's soldiers, reducing their ability to fight off infection. One does not get ill immediately after getting infected with HIV if the body is well nourished. The virus can remain quiet for five to ten years in the body before any observable signs and symptoms manifest."

"How can I know that I have AIDS?" asked Yebo-Yebo.

"It is not very easy to know immediately, unless you have been diagnosed HIV positive by blood tests, because the signs and symptoms are like those of the flu, as we have said," replied the Counsellor.

"I had all the signs and symptoms that you mentioned, Sister, and the doctor took my blood, and he has told me that I am HIV Positive," replied Yebo-Yebo. "What can I do now, and how should I live with this virus? I am scared, worried and ashamed."

"That is why I am here, so that we can talk about this," responded the Counsellor. "Yebo-Yebo, you need to treat this like any chronic disease such as cancer, diabetes, or hypertension. Don't take it as a death sentence," she continued.

"Present yourself as a healthy, confident person. Talk to someone you trust, such as a family member, trusted friend, your sexual partner, and you can also trust and be open to me as your Counsellor. Confidentiality will be ensured.

"Mix with people and live a normal and purposeful life. Have plans and goals, and strive to achieve them. Please do know that all HIV/AIDS sufferers need a lot of support and counselling from their families, relatives, community and society at large, so don't cut them off from your life.

"HIV/AIDS sufferers are not to be discriminated against, but accepted as individuals suffering from any chronic disease.

"That is why I am motivating you to accept the situation in which you are, and live a normal life, for as long as you can.

"Take care of your sexual behaviour and your health, and consider the following factors: -

"Abstain from sexual intercourse, and use a condom if sex is unavoidable; have one partner who already knows about you; and prevent pregnancy, as the child would be infected too.

"Regarding diet, eat a balanced diet with additional proteins like meat, chicken, fish, eggs, beans, milk and soya foods. Eat fruit and vegetables for vitamins and mineral salts. If your appetite becomes poor, reduce animal fat, and rather use vegetable fat.

"If diarrhoea develops, drink a lot of cold fluids and seek the doctor's help. Observe hygiene. Wash your body, and keep your skin intact, to avoid outside infection. Cover your wounds, sores and cuts thoroughly. Control bleeding, and don't let your blood get in contact with anybody.

"Don't share underwear. Treat any genitalia discharges immediately.

"Do exercises, and keep yourself active. Choose a suitable sport of your choice. Get acquainted to taking walks, doing gardening and any household activities, and join community projects too.

"Keep yourself busy, to prevent brooding, boredom and self-pity by doing handwork, recreational activities and socialisation.

"Gain courage and acceptance and counsel others regarding prevention and coping with the disease.

"Give yourself enough rest.

"Take precautions to prevent other infections by avoiding being in contact with infectious people; unhealthy environments that are cold and draughty; and avoiding contaminated food and water.

"Promptly treat any minor infections like colds, flu and sores.

"Identify early signs and symptoms of complications in your health condition, and seek medical and Nurse's help, as it might be an indication that full-blown AIDS has developed.

"Take your medication as prescribed by the doctor.

"Get to know available resources like HIV/AIDS Counselling Clinics. AIDS counsellors, hospitals, and religious groups for sharing ideas and experiences. Also know NGO's catering for HIV/AIDS victims.

"People at these numbers are also helpful: -
**National AIDS Help Line – 0800 012322**
**Lovelife – 0800 121900**

Yebo-Yebo told his mother of his diagnosis on her next visit to the hospital. He also made an arrangement with his Counsellor to speak to her about all the support and acceptance they needed to give him as a family, so that he could accept and cope with his present situation.

He told her that he had been advised that counselling should not be focussed on HIV/AIDS sufferers or victims only, but to all community members as well, so that the fears of victims in their struggle for acceptance and coping can be allayed. They need our genuine moral support, understanding and care.

When HIV/AIDS sufferers know that the world is not ashamed of them, they can walk proudly knowing that they are not alone.

When they know they are not discriminated against, they can withstand opportunistic infections.

When they know they are protected, they can be strong and face the fatal disease.

When they know that care can be administered to them, they can feel the warmth and love of their community.

When they know there is hope for their children, they can rest assured that they will not feel maligned.

When they know they are cherished and loved, they can defeat the fear, denial and stigma associated with AIDS.

When they know they are embraced, they can stand up and be open about their status.

When they know there is no one pointing a finger at them, they can feed their systems no more with different kinds of medication.

When they know they are not isolated, they can withstand all odds, and break the silence.

When they know that the veil of stigma has disappeared, they can defeat the pain that eats them.

When their dignity and human rights are not trampled upon, their strength, wisdom, courage and power will be ignited.

When they know that the stain of being marginalized is totally non-existent, they will feel the light that their community shines around them - and they will feel brighter.

When they know that the walls of isolation have truly crumbled, care and support will be the greatest love of all.

Yebo-Yebo's mother watched her son put his hands together as he prayed, "Lord, they care," and knew that the information the Counsellor had given would make a difference in their lives. Yebo-Yebo felt a burning hope for a cure for AIDS and then prayed for that too.

# Alcoholism

By Phasekile Radebe

Alcohol is a much-loved beverage by a good number of South African citizens, as well as by people throughout the world. People consume and adore it without consideration of its after effects, when taken excessively. It is for this reason that we need to discuss this problem openly and deeply to educate and enlighten our fellow brethren. So how can we define alcoholism to everybody's understanding?

Alcoholism simply means excessive drinking or dependence on alcohol, leading to psychological aberrations or interference with the physical and mental health of the victim, strained interpersonal relationships; as well as dysfunctional social and economic behaviour.

An alcoholic has clearly identifiable features that really cannot be missed, namely:-

Drinking compulsively without restraint;

Chronic drinking and history of drinking over a long period of time;

The person drinks until intoxicated;

The alcoholic drinks in an erratic fashion, like drinking excessively over weekends, and the effect of the alcohol has a negative influence on his/her interpersonal functioning.

A classification can also be made according to an individual's drinking patterns.

There are people who do not drink alcoholic beverages at all, and these people are called "Total Abstainers".

"Social Drinkers" are those who consume a certain amount of alcohol at social gatherings, with no intention of getting intoxicated, while, "Sporadic Excessive Drinkers" drink occasionally but get intoxicated when they do.

"Heavy Social Drinkers" drink frequently, especially

at social events, and are always in the company of people who get intoxicated.

Then there are the "Alcoholics". These are the "Alcohol-Lords", who drink heavily and are really dependent upon alcohol. If they try to abstain, they show withdrawal signs.

Let us remember that no one is born an alcoholic. Alcoholism is a learned behavioural problem. There are many factors that lead to alcoholism, things like disappointments and failures in life, for example, failure to achieve a certain goal; or broken promises like engagements; loss of income, as in unemployment or poverty; loss of a loved one, as in death; family disintegration, separation and divorce, leaving a person with no sense of belonging; feelings of insecurity, leading people to consume alcohol to boost their ego, as seen in timid people.

Violence in homes and communities does make people resort to alcohol. Alcoholism can also be inherited, where parents drink freely in front of their children, who in turn, believe that it is the right thing to do, whereas it is not so.

The issue of alcoholism reminds me of Thomas and Timothy, who were old school friends during their teenage, and they were both "Total Abstainers".

Tom continued with his academic education and became a doctor. Tim dropped out of school, and ended up not getting permanent jobs, and then took to booze. After many years, they met in Johannesburg, and Tom was surprised and disappointed at Tim's condition. He was drunk and shabby, speaking foul language, presenting all signs of an alcoholic.

"Hello, Tim, how are you?" greeted Tom.

"Can't...can't you see I'm as fit as a fiddle?" responded Tim, staggering.

"I want to talk to you, my friend. Please visit me at Zola No 7 on Monday evening," said Tom.

Indeed Tim went to Tom's residence as requested.

Tom had prepared dinner but Tim ate very little. Tom offered him coffee, but Tim refused it, and demanded brandy. At that moment he was having tremors. Tom realised that his friend was addicted to alcohol.

"Tim, let us talk about alcoholics," said Tom.

"Speak, Lord, your servant will listen," responded Tim sarcastically.

Tom started his counselling lecture, and as he continued, he was surprised to see Tim was listening attentively.

"I want to tell you about the ill effects of excessive alcohol consumption, my friend," he said, avoiding telling Tim that he already suspected him of being an alcoholic.

"People who drink a lot become dependant on alcohol and become alcoholics," Tom went on. "It is pathetic how their lives become ruined. Socially, alcoholics have poor moral standards. They have no sexual inhibitions; they go about exposing their sexual organs in public, and relieving themselves anywhere. They have no shame. Alcoholics often engage in fights, and have confrontations with the law. They are a danger to the public. They are not road-worthy drivers; they always cause accidents due to their poor concentration. They generally use abusive language," continued Tom, in an advisory tone.

"Alcoholics' families disintegrate, leading to separation and even divorce. The suicide rate amongst alcoholics is very high, as they, alcoholics, invariably have feelings of insecurity and of not being loved. They raise an incidence of child abuse physically, emotionally, educationally and sexually. Alcoholic parents become poor role models to their children, and this creates a vicious cycle. Because of feelings of insecurity, children of alcoholics end up as 'street children', 'delinquents', and 'muggers'. Economically, alcoholics fail to maintain financial equilibrium. They fail to meet the needs of people committed to their care. They cannot provide food, clothes, education, shelter, and then their children take to the streets."

Tom was surprised to see that Tim was still very attentive, so he went on.

"At work, alcoholics show poor work-performance, and hence they are less productive. Their rate of absenteeism is very high. They are prone to injuries at work, and therefore are a hazard to Workman's Compensation. Alcoholics are always in conflict with their co-workers, supervisors and employers. Physically, many of their systems are affected. Mainly the gastro-intestinal tract, presenting itself in the form of mouth ulcers; oesophageal ulcers; diarrhoea; vomiting; gastritis and haemorrhoids. These conditions can lead to mal-absorption of foods, manifesting itself at the end as pellagra. Heavy drinking causes poor heart muscle tone, leading to cardiac failure and hypertension. It can also affect the muscular and skeletal system, leading to severe peripheral neuritis and contraction of the limbs, until the person is completely handicapped and unable to walk."

Tim immediately stood up, tested his legs to see if he could still walk, took a few jumps, sat down again and listened.

"The liver and the pancreas also get affected," continued Tom. "Carbohydrates metabolism gets impaired, resulting in alcoholic-pancreatitis, alcoholic-hepatitis, and a blown up abdomen (ascites), and eventually, cancer of both the liver and pancreas. Diabetes Mellitus then sets in too.

"The reproductive system likewise gets affected. Men get shrinkage of testes, and they lack sexual power (impotence). Females get menstrual disturbances and frigidity. This can lead to accusations of unfaithfulness from partners, ending up in marital problems."

"Is that so, my friend?" exclaimed Tim, his eyes wide open.

"Yes, it is so," responded Tom, "and that is not all. The mental system, the central nervous system, also gets affected," continued Tom.

"Alcoholics show aggressive behaviour. They can

go out on a fighting spree (crazy drunk) and regret it fully the following day. They become very violent, and like arguments. They sometimes suffer with anxiety, depression, and nervousness, and these changes in the mood can lead to suicidal tendencies, because of feelings of guilt and failure to perform. Alcoholics also get delirium tremens, that is 'shakes and shivers' caused by withdrawal. They suffer loss of memory (amnesia) and impaired concentration and thinking. Their brains eventually get ruined."

"Tom, you are scaring me. Is there any treatment for alcoholism?" asked Tim.

"Yes, Tim, there is help for this condition, but first an alcoholic must realise and accept that he or she has a problem, and needs help. It is unfortunate that an alcoholic has a very strong defence mechanism of denial; therefore, he or she must take a leading and active role in their own rehabilitation programme.

"The alcoholic must be made aware of the available resources like Alcoholics Anonymous (AA), South African National Council of Alcoholics (SANCA), Halfway Houses and sheltered employment facilities and so on. If these facilities fail, the alcoholic may need institutionalisation in a psychiatric hospital, clinic or rehabilitation centre. The family needs help too. They must face reality that an alcoholic needs help. They need to co-operate and assist him in his rehabilitation process. Resentment and neglect can only re-enforce the reasons why the individual decided to drink initially. Children of the alcoholics can be helped through the social welfare services to get their welfare needs."

"Tom, do you think I am an alcoholic too?" asked Tim.

"I did not say so," replied Tom, "but if you think you fit in many of the things we have discussed, then you do need help immediately."

"Tom, please take me to an A.A. tomorrow," requested Tim in a disturbed manner. It was very fortunate that Tim realised that he had a problem. He started his rehabilitation programme, and continued successfully until he no longer needed alcohol. He was very grateful to his friend Thomas.

I have no doubt that if alcohol could write its own CV (Curriculum Vitae), it would say: -

*I am Mr Alcohol*
*I am more powerful than the combined armies of the world.*
*I have destroyed more men than all the wars of the nations.*
*I am more deadly than bullets, and I have wrecked more homes than the mightiest of guns.*
*I am the world's slyest thief; I steal millions of rands each year.*
*I spare no one, and I find my victims among the rich and poor alike.*
*The young and the old, the strong and the weak, widows and orphans know me.*
*I loom up to such proportions that I cast my shadow over every field of labour.*
*I lurk in unseen places and do most of my work silently.*
*You are warned against me but you heed not.*
*I am relentless.*
*I am everywhere, in the home, on the street, in the factory,*
*In the office, on the sea and in the air.*
*I bring sickness, degradation and death, and yet,*
*Few seek to destroy me.*
*I destroy and crush; I give nothing, and take all;*
*I am your worst enemy*
*"I am Mr Alcohol"*

# Know Your Frame Of Mind "Personality Trait"

By Phasekile Radebe

A chameleon changes its colour to match its environment, as a protective measure. Likewise, human beings change their characteristic ways of thinking and acting as an effort to adapt to their environment or situation. This change includes personal characteristics, values, motives, genetic-factors, attitudes, emotional reactivity, abilities, self-image, and intelligence. It also includes a person's visual behavioural patterns.

All these factors influence changes in our frames of mind at that moment in time. Basically, we all have three "personality traits", "characteristics", or "frames of mind", namely Parent Frame of Mind, which can either be "critical" or "nurturing".

Did you know that at times we possess, and act or think with a "Child Frame of Mind" which can either be "rebellious", "helpless" or "free"? And at other times we can also act or behave in our "Adult Frame of Mind".

Remember this is not referring to an adult, a parent or a child. We can all have any of these personality traits, irrespective of age, depending on situations we are faced with *at that moment*. I have no doubt we all wish to know how we behave at different times, and how other people view us as individuals during those changes.

**The Parent Frame of Mind.** The "Critical Parent Frame of Mind," at this phase, we look at things and life with a very critical eye. We become very restrictive and paranoid. We make demands that are unfounded. Do you remember when you say to your friends or your family members, or even to your children, "I do not want you to do that!" or "I do not want you to make friends with that so and so – he is no good" or "he is not of your class!" This is acting on the capacity of what *you* want, rather than the needs of the next person.

We become very judgemental, and get ourselves influenced by our obstinate opinions. At that moment, we have frowning dispositions, and point fingers of accusation towards other people. Many a time, we then act aggressively when ignored, when in reality, we want to be listened to.

It is easy to classify this characteristic as mean and bossy, but in reality, it is not as bad as it may seem. It has its good qualities too. It provides order and structure when things get out of hand; it keeps control; it has knowledge of identifying right from wrong; and is thus strongly protective and has quick answers. It may seem harsh and unnecessary, but it does have good principles.

How then does the "Nurturing Parent Frame of Mind" portray itself? This is when we are very concerned and caring about other people or situations. It is when we are compassionate and considerate about what other people are experiencing; when we are loving and warmly protective. We have our arms open to those who are hurting, and willingly offer to be involved in the healing process of their wounds and stress. It is when we have a sentimental tone with a smiling and accepting facial expression.

In the dimension of our **"Child Frame of Mind"**, we think and act in our child perspective. We may be in our "Rebellious–Child Frame of Mind", the "Helpless Child Frame of Mind", or the "Free Child's Mind" depending on our behaviour. How then do we behave in our "Rebellious Child Frame of Mind?"

We react rebelliously and negatively to suggestions and proposals even before we consider and analyse their merits.

We don't welcome advice, and we consider ourselves to be always perfect, and we undermine other people's integrity.

Our "Helpless Child Frame of Mind" reacts very helplessly to other people, and to our tasks.

We cannot take our responsibilities responsibly and effectively. In fact, we act very dependently on other people or parents, if any. We always expect to be told what to do, how and when. We are non-assertive and very pessimistic. We are inadequate and incapable, easily submissive, and never offer opposition to suggestions or directives. We fail to make decisions of our own, or saying straight and frankly what we want, need, or what we don't want or need.

What then about our "Free Child Frame of Mind?"

Here is when we are free, creative, enthusiastic, and spontaneous. We are full of energy, and have free response to challenges and life. We are gracefully natural, with open minds and trust other people. We openly and directly express our feelings and emotions. We are also overflowing with energy, and are in high spirits. We don't allow stress to overpower us. We aim to go on with our lives positively.

We also at times behave in our "**Adult Frame of Mind**". Here we think and act from our 'adult-self'. We are able to check our facts, and sort out problems. (Problem Solving Ability.) We think and make our plans with sober judgment. Our adult frame of mind gives us ability to evaluate and appropriately respond to each situation.

In this frame of mind, we like to think, learn and figure things out. It is that part of us that likes to deal with the world's events and facts objectively. It helps us to look ahead, calculate possibilities, and make decisions rationally.

Our adult frame of mind looks at the world unemotionally. Here we construct our understandings and take decisions with the consideration to possible progressive outcome. Our adult self can serve as a co-ordinator between the moral demands of our "parent" and our "child" frame of mind. It can make situation-analysis on what can work, and what cannot work, very constructively. It has the ability to face life's challenges positively.

This frame of mind can work independently, but because of its good qualities of moderation and co-ordination, it likes to work interdependently with our "parent" and our "child" frame of mind, to form a control system.

It helps the "parent" mind in us, especially the critical parent, to assess and evaluate our very strict control measure, and move with the times. It can also help our "child" frame of mind to get a role model.

In our adult frame of mind, we can train ourselves to be knowledgeable about our own morals, and the morals of other people, and face stressful and traumatic challenges positively. (Optimistic).

It will be interesting for each of us to analyse our behavioural patterns in order to determine which one works better for us and other people (win-win). We each may be having our own criteria for this analysis, but the following questionnaire may also help.

Does your frame of mind support and strengthen your own and other people's dignity, or does it reduce it?

Is your frame of mind based on objective reality acceptable to other people, or is it based on your negative imagination?

Does your frame of mind help you to reach your most deeply held goals and values successfully?

Does your frame of mind help you to minimise your personal and social conflict? If your answers are positive, your personality is likely to be a "Clear Thinking Adult Frame of Mind". Assessing and understanding the above personality traits can help us to know more about ourselves. We can also know why other people react or act the way they do towards us, and then we can sort out our behavioural problems where necessary, to promote peace and stability.

# The Song of Parental Love

By Phasekile Radebe

The mother was looking at her baby and eventually said, "I looked after you so well for nine full months while you were still in utero, and it did not matter whether you were a boy or a girl. I went to the clinics for the nurses' and doctors' advice.

"I tried, with success, to follow their education and instructions like:

Avoid stress and strain,
Avoid beverages with alcohol,
Don't smoke,
Do mild exercise and rest,
Go to the clinic when you notice any drainages of water or stains of blood,
Go to the hospital immediately when there is bleeding or contractions,
Go to the clinic on your regular clinic days for assessment, and so on.

"I will continue looking after you even now that you are born, all the way through your growing stages. I will feed you, love you and nurture you.

"I will teach you socialisation and personality skills even before you get global skills from your peers, teachers, and community at large. I will give you a good up-bringing to enable you to make better choices with your body, your mind, your love, your hates, your abilities, and your interests, and to make better decisions about your actions, and reactions, your behaviour and your attitudes.

"There are common features in the biological aspect of men that you must reach and appreciate. There is a phrase which says – I quote: '*Man is a social being, born with social needs common to most men, therefore he must adjust himself to a condition of interdependency with other members of his society. No man is therefore born to live in isolation.'* These are true words to remember always in life."

Parents should remember that in early stages, the child imitates you 'the parent' in the socialisation process. As he grows, he becomes an evaluating organism, with the ability to sift and select models he wants to follow.

We therefore define 'child-rearing' as a process that involves transmitting to the child through training and example the models of behaviour and values, which are culturally acceptable, thus enabling him to become an adjusted and effective member of his society.

Socialisation of the child in rearing starts with very simple and normal stages namely:

*Oral Stage* – that is gratification that the child gets through breast-feeding, which contributes the early socialisation (mother/child relationship). That is why breast-feeding is highly recommended.

*Toilet Training Stage* – This signifies a stage of understanding direction and instructions.

*Latency Stage* – This is manifestation of identity. A girl starts playing with dolls, mothering them. A boy plays with car toys, and bicycles, like his father. At this stage, parents should do their best to display good role modelling.

Here, they should ensure availability of 'basic-needs' namely – sense of belonging (love), safety and security, physical care and affection, self-esteem and self-actualisation.

Grow my child; grow, the mother always comments. The truth is, every parent wishes and expects his or her child to be an asset in the family and community.

It is also unfortunate that the child can also become a deviant and disappointment to the family. The remedy is 'good parent/child relationship' and guidance. This needs collective and individual roles well played.

**Parents collectively** form the most persistent and constant factors in the child's life. Friends are dropped; playmates forgotten readily, teachers exchanged, but parents remain the most contact people from childhood to adulthood.

Parents nourish, nurture and maintain their children from infancy to adulthood.

They transmit cultural heritage, and mould the personality of their children.

They provide an atmosphere where their children may make mistakes, or prove their successes within an atmosphere of protection.

They always provide open hands for their children even when the society applies pressure.

They initiate religious perspective to their children, and instil respect, obedience, love, self-control and self-discipline.

The *mother's role* is viewed as a pillar for the whole family. This has been proved by the fact that when the father dies, mom successfully maintains the family, but when the mother dies, the whole family collapses.

The mother is the provider of all the basic needs, including education. She is observant and sensitive to the needs of the whole family. She is the comforter and supporter of all (including the father) in time of crisis.

She is held responsible for each child's deviant behaviour.

She ensures healthy conditions for the whole family, but when she is sick, she gets very little nursing care – if any at all.

Despite all these responsibilities, the husband claims all children (especially achievers) are his, except for the deviants who are hers, and have thus inherited these characteristics from her.

The *father's role* is to give the family a name, security, discipline, protection, and to dictate orders and family rules very authoritatively within the family. He is an ultimate ruler; hence men are threatened by 'gender-equality'.

**The Home As A Good Model:**
Bring me up under correct guidance of a loving home, then I will have no desire to wander away in search of pleasure, and outside companionship.

Evil will not easily attract me.

The atmosphere of love that prevails within the family will mould my character.

I will maintain good habits and principles that create strong defence against temptations when I leave home-shelter, and proudly take my stand in the society, and the world at large.

You have grown my child, but always remember the profound truth of the old proverb, which says, "It takes a village to raise a child."

You are a product of the community in which you grew up.

Your parents gave you your biological constitution. Your family reared you, but that wider village, town or city made its impact on you. You benefit from its strength, and you suffer from its limitations. You are also shaped by some of these limitations.

Always give it your full consideration and support. In your thoughts and prayers, always say, "Thank you, Lord, for the community from which I come. Help me to be a part of the solution to its problems, and a contribution to its hope for the future."

# As Tough as a Woman

By Gloria Gladys Khanyile

The attitude of in-laws to their daughter-in-law (*umakoti*) remains tense. The latter still has to undergo a severe test. Some in-laws do it with the intention of even ending the relationship between their son and his wife. The response of the daughter-in-law sometimes depends on how her husband handles the situation and how she uses the counselling she was given at home before she got married.

Traditionally, a girl is counselled by an older person in the family, usually her granny, about the difficulties she is likely to encounter in her new family. She is called by her granny, to sit and listen to her counselling (*ukuyala*). This is done so that she exercises patience and the ability to overcome problems.

Zodwa, who was married, was not accepted by all the in-laws, except the father, because they had had somebody else in mind and were even closer to the family of that particular woman.

Zodwa first stayed with her husband's family and endured all sorts of insulting remarks. So they rented a room not so far away from her in-laws' home, as at the time, it was not easy to immediately have their own house.

This was convenient for the in-laws. Her sisters-in-law, particularly, and some brothers-in-law visited them frequently and continued to insult Zodwa there. The owners of the house where they rented their room were an elderly couple, who where thankful to have this young couple staying with them.

This elderly couple would overhear the insults directed at Zodwa, and they became a source of comfort, and would give Zodwa all the support and advice she needed.

When Zodwa was expecting her second child, her husband decided to buy a site and build a house.

Unfortunately, this place was also not so far away from his home. As soon as the house was finished and Zodwa and her husband about to move into it, the mother-in-law and her family were furious, and said Zodwa did not deserve to have a house and *they* wanted to move into the new house. The problem with her husband was that he was too soft and allowed his family to do and say anything to Zodwa to hurt her.

To this, Zodwa said to her husband, "Alright, let them all move to the new house and we take the old one." Whatever happened thereafter, Zodwa never got to know, but her husband told her to pack their belongings and move to their new house.

They moved into their new house immediately, and not one of her in-laws even came to visit them in their new home for some time, but Zodwa found out that they visited when she was away at work.

One day, the younger brother-in-law was getting married. On the day of the wedding, they all got dressed up and left for the church leaving Zodwa alone to cook for the wedding. She, together with two of their neighbors, who had come to help, did all the cooking, table setting and preparations successfully. From then on, they realised how worthy Zodwa was. But to them, she remained just good enough to rely on whenever there was hard work to be done. Whenever they had traditional parties, they would all sit together, chat and gossip and wait for Zodwa to do all the cooking. After eating, they would sit and relax with hard drinks and beers with their friends, while Zodwa did all the washing up.

The tough Zodwa remained undistracted; she formed a woman's club with her friends. They took lessons in sewing, flower arranging, cooking and catering. Whenever anyone of them had a party or any form of occasion, they would work together and produce a high standard of performance.

Zodwa by now had three children, two daughters and

a son. Her children attended Module C schools and she needed transport to take them to school. At first, she arranged for transport to take them to and from school.

Her husband had a car but he told her he was unable to take their children to school. In the meantime, his mother forced him to take care of the illegitimate children of his sisters and see to their schooling. So Zodwa's husband found himself doing more for these illegitimate children than his own.

Zodwa started driving lessons and when she got a driver's license, she bought herself a car and took her children to and from school for all their schooling years, until they had to go to universities.

Despite her busy schedule, Zodwa also managed to study. In the afternoon, over and above the house chores, she had to help all her children with homework and had her own assignments to write. Their father, who was a teacher by profession, was never there to help with the children's homework.

Zodwa was involved in many activities including the church and the club. No one knew just how she managed all these. She was so busy, and equally as tense, but more than anything else, she was determined to succeed in whatever she set out to do. She was a good dressmaker, and expert in flower arranging just to mention a few of her successes.

By the time Zodwa's two daughters started work, one had completed her honors in B. Comm. and the other her B Comm. degree. The youngest child, her son, was doing his third year in a Chartered Accounting Degree, and Zodwa had become a senior lecturer at one of the universities. She received her doctorate.

Zodwa did not only motivate her children, she also motivated her husband, who also received a doctorate and became a professor at another university. He started participating more in his family affairs, but sadly, the in-laws never stopped being nasty to Zodwa, whenever they get a chance.

Zodwa became more relaxed as she started to reap the rewards of her hard work.
As tough as a woman.

# The Pre-Democratic Life In The Township

By Barbara Gumede

If I were to describe a township in my own words, I would say it was a vast land with matchbox houses, looking unfinished, as they were not plastered, had no electricity, no water inside the house barring a tap outside, with toilets outside in the yard.

These were two bed-roomed with no doors, the owner having to hang curtains to try to create some privacy. The dining room and kitchen were also very small. The bathroom was a shower in the toilet away from the house. There wasn't much space between houses; you could hear all the conversations from your neighbour. No other race was allowed to live there excepting Bantu, meaning black people, as they were known at that time.

People did not stay for free in these houses. They paid rent. Although the houses did not cost much, it made no difference as there was no money. Those employed earned next to nothing.

I remember, one day, after my husband had gone to work I was left alone with my son, who was eight months old then. I heard footsteps coming toward my house. I peeped through the window and saw municipal police coming. We had not paid our rent and they were coming to lock the house. The procedure was if you didn't pay your rent on time, you would be evicted, the house would be locked, and then re-opened only when you had paid.

I got under the bed with my child praying that he did not cry, because if they found me I would be in trouble. My baby was quiet. They locked us in and went away. I got out from under the bed and sang, "Hallelujah!"

I prepared the evening meal. Just then, I heard my husband talking to himself, "Where have they gone to?"

I ran to the door and told him the police locked us in

because the rent had not been paid. He went to the township office to pay and the house was reopened.

There were many disadvantages forced on people in the township. There were no shops, no playgrounds for the children, no clinics and very few schools. Shopping was done in town from Indian and white shops. We were not allowed to go inside the white shop.

This practice wisened blacks to do things for themselves. Mothers learned to sew clothes for their families and sold some. Others resorted to selling and brewing African beer in their back yards. Police raided them day and night, as it was illegal to sell beer. Woman thought of many tricks to protect their beer from being spoiled by police. Some dug holes in their back yard and the beer was covered with soil.

During a raid, police would look for beer and never find it. Though the smell was there, they never discovered where it came from. After the raid, customers would come back and enjoy themselves because they knew that once the police had raided they wouldn't come back again until the next day.

This practice of selling beer led to a lot of competition. It is where the gangsters and murderers were formed, and they were known as "*olayitha*" meaning "the enlightened one". If you wanted to install electricity or a phone, you were told this was not your property and therefore you were not to attempt to do anything.

Ironing was done by using a primus stove to heat the iron, and our studies were done by candlelight.

Stockvel was another form of entertainment and also generating money. Members of the stockvel were considered the elite group in the community. They dressed well and had money.

That era has now passed and a new one has set in - the war humanity has against HIV/AIDS. It is ravaging the country like wild fire. How can we conquer this enemy? Education is one way; abstinence or condomising is another.

Only time will tell. Drug abuse is another enemy that has taken and is taking many young lives, targeting schools and the unemployed youth.

# The Beautiful Valley Where I Grew Up

By Gloria Gladys Khanyile

I was born at Mariannhill near Pinetown over sixty years ago. Mariannhill is a Catholic Mission which was established in 1882 by Father Francis Abbot. The mission was divided into different areas and each given names. Some of the names were biblical, like Emmaus and Nazareth. I grew up in Nazareth, which is the area nearest to Pinetown.

This was a sparsely populated valley and all of the families living there knew one another. The climate was wonderful. The rains started early in spring and were regular throughout summer. It was hot in summer but there were no extremes of heat. Though it was cold in winter, it was never unbearable. My granny used to tell us about the snow in winter in Mooi River where she was born, but we never witnessed it here.

Religion here was one hundred percent Catholic. Residence here was only given to our people if they were converted to Catholicism. There were no formal social activities except cultural performances and weddings. Sundays were for attending church services and those that had joined the Mother's Union attended their meetings at least once a month on Sundays and every Thursday. Sundays were enjoyed as people enjoyed dressing up smartly for Church. As for Christmas Day, most of the people especially the children and the youth wore brand new dresses and suits. During the summer holidays our family went to the beach in Durban and also visited a few areas of entertainment there. This was most enjoyable. Black people were forbidden to drink western drinks, that is, beers and hot stuff. They were not allowed anywhere near a bottlestore except those, who were exempted (*amazemtiti*) meaning they had to apply to carry a special card allowing them access to the bottle store.

Black people had to entertain themselves with Zulu beer, and even those amounts were restricted in their daily life. I am not sure if this restriction came from the mission or it was law. All I remember is a permit certificate my uncle had. It allowed him to make four gallons of Zulu beer at a time. An increased amount was allowed for celebrations.

As there were few families, each household had vast areas of land to themselves. Fortunately, people then were industrious and they took pride in ploughing the land. Almost all families had a kraal with cattle and goats. Some had more than others. Very few did not have cattle and were looked at as odd. However, every home had fowls.

There was plenty of vacant lands, bushes, tall grass and forests plus food in the fields. This attracted such animals as rabbits, springboks and monkeys, which moved fairly freely in the area. But there were also dogs in some of the homes. The boys would set their dogs on these animals. The only thing that saved them from being savaged by dogs was their speed.

We had fruit trees like pawpaws and mangoes, and monkeys came uphill from the forest to steal, particularly the pawpaws. I remember one day we saw the male and female monkeys climbing up the pawpaw tree while their young looked on from beneath the tree. We chased them down the hill carrying sticks. A male must have noticed that we were all young and he just stopped abruptly, communicated with the females, who in response quickly pulled their young down into the forest. The male casually put down the pawpaw he was carrying and challenged us to come to him. We immediately turned back uphill, screaming all the way. As we looked back to see if he was following us, he coolly took the pawpaw and slowly walked down into the forest. Beside the fruit, the monkeys also stole the mealies and pumpkins from the fields.

As there were plenty of mealies and corn (*amabele*) in the fields, there were many species of bird. Small and big ones, that flew in groups, couples and solo. All enjoying the harvest from the fields.

I was brought up by a single parent. We were a family of six - my grandmother, my mother, my three brothers and myself. I was the third born and my younger brother last. My mother was widowed young as she also married at a young age. She had to go out to work to bring us all up. This was during the Second World War and she started working at a clothing factory. They were sewing uniforms for the soldiers, which were needed urgently so they had to work overtime. As the houses had to be dark, at night during the war, it meant they had to start work very early in the morning so that they go back home early for their home chores, then put off lights at dusk.

These were hard times. Everything was scarce, but fortunately for the factory workers who were sewing for soldiers, their bosses pleaded with the government to let them have the privilege of getting some of the items, especially food, that were restricted or unavailable to ordinary people.

My grandmother remained with us at home. She was a very industrious person, who just loved ploughing the fields. She was up at four in the morning to the fields and came back around eight o clock to make us breakfast, milk cows and then take out the cattle and young goats. Each one of us was given a young goat as his or her own to look after and this taught us to love these young animals. I remember one day a local thief stole and slaughtered one of our young goats; we cried so much but were happy that he was arrested and jailed for the crime.

Granny would go back to the fields for most of the day and only come back to make supper. My two elder brothers would help by getting the cattle and goats back home when they came back from school. Throughout the year, we had plenty of milk and sour milk (*maas*) as there were many cows. Maas was stored in big calabashes (*amagula*), each having a hole at the bottom that was closed with a spigot. On re-opening the spigot, the whey would be drained out and only delicious cream Maas remained in the calabash. Maas was added to cooked mealie meal (*uphuthu*) or my Granny would boil dry mealies (*izinkobe*), grind it and mix with Maas to eat.

As there were plenty of fowls, there were lots of eggs to eat but my mother preferred to buy more eggs from the nearby poultry farm so that there were more fowls for their meat. In summer there was plenty of mealies, pumpkin and vegetables, all home grown. My granny also planted groundnuts (*izindlubu*), sweet potatoes and gems (*amandmbe*). I remember on a cold rainy day, Granny would wake up early in the morning to reap green mealies, pumpkins, pumpkin leaves and tomatoes; she would come back home and make a fire in the kitchen using big stems of dry wood so that the fire burned the whole day making the kitchen very warm. Then she would put a big three-legged pot on the fire with first, layers of fresh mealies, then on top of the mealies, huge pieces of pumpkin and added water. This would cook in no time and she would then dish it out for us. As we sat and enjoyed this around the fireplace, she would be grinding more mealies on her grindstone.

She would wash and cut the pumpkin leaves and tomatoes, add them to the mealie dough, finally adding salt and pepper. She would then take and wash the mealie leaves, and wrap this around the prepared dough. She used mealie stems cut to short sticks and laid them at the bottom of the pot then put the prepared wrapped dough on this base. Finally, she would add water to the pot and cook this. This is called Mealie Bread and it is delicious.

We would spend the rest of the day chatting excitably, laughing and singing. Sadly though, my mother would be out at work until late in the afternoon, sometimes even later in the evening, when the Umbilo River was full and she had to take a longer distance to cross the river, where the only bridge was. She would come back to a warm house with all of the meals ready prepared by my granny.

The missionary provided good education and each one of us started schooling as soon as we reached school age.

The school was quite a distance from home as it took an hour of brisk walking to reach there. There was no road leading to the school. We had to walk along the path downhill, on straight, then uphill, downhill again and finally uphill to get to the road that would take us there. It provided good exercise, we were quite fit and I loved every minute of the journey. The teachers at school were well disciplined and committed to their work. If every parent co-operated and disciplined their children, everybody would have benefited greatly. Unfortunately, few reached higher education.

As the population gradually increased, those vast areas of land had to be reduced so that more people would be accommodated. As more industries were established nearby Pinetown, the younger lot mostly preferred working at the industries rather than continuing with education or ploughing fields. Almost at the same time, came the rumours that the land was going to be taken away from the people, therefore they should do away with their livestock. People sold some, and slaughtered some of their cattle. Indeed, some families in areas of Nazareth started to move away before they were ordered to. Most of the land stood forlorn and neglected.

Then came the time of uprising. People called meetings to resist removal until eventually they won. The place was soon developed for building proper houses and more houses. Each household was appointed a small area around the house and the rest of the land was used to build yet more houses.

Today, Nazareth is a crowded noisy place with a lot of strangers as neighbors, and of course, crime is on the increase. On the positive side, there is now a crèche and a primary school. There is good transport to commute workers and scholars. Above all, there is now electricity and clean water from taps.

It is an ill wind that blows nobody any good!

# On Her Majesty's Coronation

By Gloria Gladys Khanyile

It was way back in 1953, exactly fifty years ago, when I went to college at Marianhill St Francis College, to do Standard Seven, which was then called Standard Eight or Form II.

We were just getting adjusted to boarding school life when a few of us were called to the Principal's office. We were told that we were going to act in a play for the Coronation of the now Queen Elizabeth II of England.

We did not know where this was going to take place as the coronation was to take place so far away in England. Later, we got to know that this was going to take place at the Durban City Hall. Imagine the excitement as we looked forward to going out on a trip to Durban!

Various schools were to present plays and sketches, some of which were fairy tales, comedies, tragedies, you name it, but all were in the spirit of celebration.

While our infant school presented a lovely fairytale, we, at the College presented a beautiful tragedy.

We were given the parts that we were to act. Six of us in our early teens, short and tiny, were to act as bees. Our attire was a pair of knickers with a top and a pair of wings all in mustard and brown stripes. When we fitted the sewn attire, we really looked like bees.

There were six tall and slender girls, who were going to wear long yellow gowns, carrying long yellow sticks and they were going to act as the rays of the sun.

Twelve older girls acted as Zulu maidens wearing short beaded skirts and little tops. These were going to accompany a young beautiful woman who acted the part of the bride (*umakoti*). The bride wore a full skin skirt (*isidwaba*), a little top with plenty of beads over her shoulders and across the chest, and a beaded traditional headgear (*isicholo*).

On the other hand, there was the bridegroom (*umkhwenyane*), wearing a skin (*ibheshu*) with beads over his shoulders and crossing his chest and a skin headband. He was accompanied by twelve young men, also wearing skin (*amabheshu*) and skin headbands.

We rehearsed our parts to perfection, and on the day of the celebration we headed for the Durban City Hall to perform the play. Unfortunately, we were not to see other plays performed by other schools. We were kept out until it was our turn, which was quite late at night.

The play started with a big wedding of the bride and bridegroom. There was a lot of singing and dancing of the young men and maidens with women ululating throughout the ceremony. Soon thereafter war broke out. The young men together with the newly-wed husband had to leave to fight in the war. The husband sadly had to bid farewell to his wife.

The young wife together with the maidens remained behind but life had to go on. They had to carry out their home chores. This was all done with singing and dancing. Fetching the water from the river, carrying it on their heads and moving back home was all done with rhythmic swaying movements. Fetching firewood, cementing the floors with mud (*ukugandaya*), and smearing them with cow dung (*ukusinda*) were all done in song and action.

Days went by, months went by, but warriors did not come back from war. The young wife got more worried by the day and eventually vocalized her fears. Still there was no return of her husband.

She instructed the bees to go and look for her husband and bring him back home. The bees circled her twice, bowed and left for the woods in search of her husband. After a while, they came back empty-handed with no sign of her husband. She got very agitated and sick with worry. Soon the warriors came back carrying her dead husband on their shoulders. She screamed once, cried and fell to the ground next to her husband. She called for the rays of the sun to burn her so that she could die with her husband. The tall girls with their long yellow gowns surrounded her and simultaneously directed their long yellow sticks towards her until she died next to her husband.

At the end of the play, the whole audience in the hall spontaneously stood up in applause and excitement and clapped for a long time. It was in the early hours of the morning when we finished and we were immediately whisked back to College. A few weeks later, we were called back to the Durban City Hall for a repeat performance as our play was amongst a few chosen as winning plays. Though the Coronation was taking place a million miles away from us, the whole country, South Africa, was abuzz with excitement and action in the celebration of this great occasion, the Coronation of Queen Elizabeth II of England.

# Wounded Spirit

By Barbara Gumede

Ekwazini Hospital was very busy that night. Outside, a strong wind was blowing violently, swaying trees and rattling windows. An ambulance came to the halt outside casualty and a pregnant woman was checked into the delivery room, her husband running behind the porters.

The woman who was known as Mrs Cooke gave birth to twins, but one twin had an umbilical cord wound tightly around her neck and was suffocating. The doctor tried all he could but there was no way he could save the baby, so the baby, Stella, died.

The surviving twin was named Sylvia. Mrs Cooke looked deep into Sylvia's eyes as if searching for answers. She said to the baby, Sylvia, "She died so that you have a chance to live! She will always live within you, in your heart, and in your soul."

Sylvia turned twenty while studying Law in her second year at University. She lay on her bed trying to figure out what had gone wrong. She had failed an important test.

Her roommate and best friend then came into the room and saw that she was having a bad day.

"Are you alright? Let's go to the Café and get something to eat," encouraged Greta

"I really don't feel like eating," replied Sylvia.

"We'll get some chocolates and cakes. That always makes you feel better," said Greta.

On the way to the café Sylvia bumped into a tall handsome man.

"Oh, I am sorry," said Sylvia apologetically.

"No. You don't have to apologise. It was my fault. I should have looked where I was going."

Greta was amazed by this and passed some rude

remarks.

"Don't be rude, Greta. I am also to blame," said Sylvia.

"Don't be stupid, Sylvia, these people never look where they are going, every single one of them," snapped Greta.

"Well, Sylvia, I am sorry," the handsome man said, and walked away.

Sylvia wanted to know why Greta was so hostile toward this man.

Greta in reply said, "You surprise me, Sylvia. Why are you defending him? You are scaring me. Next you will be wanting to marry one of them."

"That's not a bad idea, Greta. I have just lost my appetite," said Sylvia, who then turned around and walked away to their room. On the way back to their room, she saw him again and apologised for the incident earlier.

"Don't worry, it is not such a big deal. But it is certainly the first time that I've bumped into and met such a pretty lady." She introduced herself as Sylvia Cooke, and he told her his name was Caleb Hoge.

"So, Caleb, what's your major?" asked Sylvia.

He told her he was a third year accounting student and she told him that she was a law student.

They found a lot in common between them. It was not uncommon for them to sit in the park and talk for what seemed forever. Mixed race relationships were met with hostility from some sections of society, their fellow students, and even their parents.

It wasn't long before they were married, much to the disgust and shame of her family.

It wasn't long before Sylvia started practicing as a human rights lawyer. She loved her work for she was helping those who did not have money make their lives bearable. This provided her with a sense of joy and accomplishment that all the money in the world could not have provided.

Caleb was working as a chartered accountant. He

was also happy in his work.

It was late afternoon and Caleb was already there, waiting for Sylvia to arrive home. He looked worried and sad, and Sylvia became anxious.

"Hi Caleb, is there anything wrong?" she asked.

"It's your mother. She was involved in a car accident this morning and I am so sorry to say she is dead."

"We have to go home then," she said.

"*We?*" Caleb said. "You want me to go home with you? To your mother's funeral? Sylvia, you know I am not welcome amongst your people. I don't want to be put in a position where I have to defend my love for you and why we got married."

"You are my family now and that makes her your mother too. You would not miss your mother's funeral, would you?" reasoned Sylvia.

Caleb was cornered, knowing there was no way out. They set out to go to Sylvia's home.

Sylvia's father was not happy to see Caleb. "What the hell is *he* doing here?" he yelled.

"He is my husband and part of this family whether you like it or not. We are going to pay our last respects to Mama."

On hearing this, Sylvia's Uncle Mark remarked, "My sister has hardly gone cold and you are fighting like spoilt teenagers. I suggest we focus on what is important here."

Sylvia was relieved and hurriedly said, "Thank you, Uncle Mark."

Cooke turned around and mumbled, "I wonder what it would have been like if Stella had lived?"

Sylvia overheard him, and asked, "Who is Stella?"

Cooke felt a shiver run down his spine. He had not wanted Sylvia to hear it. It was a secret. "Nothing. Forget what I said," he said, and walked away.

Sylvia went to their room and found Caleb relaxing. She had a firm belief that Stella was her father's mistress.

"Sweetheart, I know your father hates me but I don't

think that he is the cheating type. He loved your mother just like I love you."

Sylvia went out of the room to find her father. She was determined to find the out truth about Stella.

"Papa, I need to talk to you," she broached.

"Sylvia, I am not in the mood to talk right now."

"Get in the mood and fast, because I am looking for answers. Who is Stella? And what is the secret?" charged Sylvia, hands on hips.

"I am not going to stand here and listen to unfounded accusations," blustered Cooke, and stormed from the room.

Later that day, Sylvia was paging through her mother's album when she found a poem. Curiosity overcame her and she read it.

*'You'll never be her and you know it too*
*Because she was my Stella*
*Your soul will stay with me forever*
*You will be with the one that lives'*

She was now even more confused. She took the poem back to her room and gave it to Caleb to read, saying, "I was looking through some of Mama's belongings and I came across this."

"It is beautiful. Who wrote it?"

"Mama wrote it."

After dinner, Sylvia and Caleb went to their room. Sylvia was tense and quiet. She cried and finally fell asleep. She had a dream. She was running away from a dark figure, whose face she could not see. Finally, she turned around to face this dark figure, and demanded, "Who are you, and what do you want from me?"

The dark figure said, "My name is Stella. I want a chance to live. It's my turn."

At that moment she caught a glimpse of its face and she screamed. It looked like her and its voice kept on ringing in her ears. "I want to live. It's my turn." Caleb comforted her. She told him of her dream that Stella was trying to kill her and that she was her twin sister.

"I didn't know you had a sister, let alone a twin."

"Neither did I," whispered Sylvia.

Sylvia ran to her father's room in the morning before the funeral. "Papa, tell me the truth."

"I thought we could talk after the funeral," said Cooke.

"Please, Papa, we need to do it now. We must talk this thing over," pleaded Sylvia.

Cooke sighed. "What do you want to know?"

"Everything."

"It all began on the night that you were born. It was a stormy night. Your mother went into labour and she delivered twins. Stella and you. Unfortunately, Stella did not survive because of complications that arose."

She could not believe what she was hearing. For the past twenty-eight years, her family had led her to believe she was the only child. It started to make sense to her. The hostility she detected from her mother, the poem and her father's words. It all became clear. What was she going to do?

It was a small funeral with just very close relatives, family and friends attending. That night there was heavy rain, thunder and lightning. Sylvia couldn't sleep so she decided to get some milk from the kitchen. Close to the fridge she saw a set of knives. Her eyes rested on a steak knife. She touched it and realised it was strong enough for what she was about to do. She removed it from the hook and went to the bedroom.

"Take care of him once and for all," she heard Stella's voice say.

"My mother hated you, Caleb. My father thinks our marriage was a big mistake and Stella is jealous of us. I am going to kill you and then commit suicide," Sylvia said in a trance.

Just then frightening thunder shook her to her senses and she dropped the knife and ran out of the house into the darkness of the night. Caleb followed her, making enough noise to wake up everybody in the house. When he got a glimpse of her, she was disappearing behind nearby trees. She ran as fast as she could. The branches of the trees scratched her but she did not care. The rain poured down in torrents accompanied by lightning and strong winds. She stopped to wipe the rain off her face and she remembered the bridge. She ran until she reached it. She climbed onto the side railing and sat on top, looking down.

"What are you doing? Are you trying to get yourself killed?" she heard Stella's voice shriek. "You know you are more stupid than I thought!"

"You want to destroy us! You are an evil spirit, Stella!" Sylvia cried, and threw herself off the bridge.

Her funeral was held two days later.

# Good Neighbours

By Gloria Gladys Khanyile

Richard and Oswald were good neighbours. The two men would sit for hours chatting, mostly at Richard's place outside in the garden in summer. Occasionally, they would be at Oswald's place. Richard had a habit of reading the morning newspaper in the loo. One day, as Richard was reading the paper in the loo, he felt something biting his legs, and nibbling at his flesh. He realised that fleas were crawling from the newspaper. He was so puzzled, wondering where they had come from.

This went on for some time and Richard was thinking of phoning the newspaper agency and complaining about the newspaper they supplied to him.

As his newspaper was delivered every morning at the crack of dawn and left on his front stoep, he decided he would wake up early before the paper was delivered so that he could confront the delivery boy. Unfortunately, that morning, he overslept and did not hear or see the person delivering the paper, but he *was* fortunate enough to discover the culprit.

His neighbour, Oswald, had a fluffy little dog, Snoopy, which had a habit of making Richard's front stoep an ideal place to spend the night. As Snoopy always accompanied his owner to Richard's place and sat with him in the garden, he must have found Richard's place more comfortable than his home. Richard discovered that Snoopy did not only sleep on his stoep but as soon as the paper was delivered, he climbed on the newspaper, which he found warmer than the stoep. By the time Richard woke up, Snoopy would be gone back to his home.

Already, Richard had been embarrassed when his guests complained of an awful itch as soon as they came to his home. The fleas were all over his house; especially the lounge, loo and bathroom, the places at which he usually read the newspaper.

Richard decided to put up a fence around his house. At the same time, he advised his neighbour to get his dog treated for fleas and advised him to buy the dog a flea collar.

The friendship of the two neighbours continued as before, but there was no more comfortable and warm bed (the newspaper) for Snoopy as there was now a fence around Richard's place. The newspaper was delivered to the post-box at the gate.

# The Misfortune of Tsepo

## by Barbara Gumede

On the foothills of Lesotho lived a very poor family. Their house was a cave with nothing inside except animal skins, which they used for clothing and blankets. Pots were made of clay and water was collected in a calabash.

There were no lights and it was dark when night fell. Everyone rushed to grab their skin blankets and a place to sleep. The places further inside the cave were favourable because of the warmth generated by the wood fire that was kept burning day and night. They ate buck meat often, as this was the only available meat. Father was a great hunter and this was the only way he could provide for his family.

Mother had some knowledge of traditional medicine. Tsepo, the eldest son was very interested in his mother's practice. He had learned a lot from her.

One day, Tsepo decided to leave his home to seek work on the neighbouring farms. His journey began at dawn, his mother having prepared some provisions of buck meat, mealie bread and water in a calabash. There was a belief that when a person travelled, they never carried uncooked meat because if they did, wild animals would be able to trace and harm them. So Tsepo carried cooked meat only.

The journey was long as he had to travel on foot, descending and ascending rocky paths. There were no roads.

It took Tsepo days to spot a smallholding in the distance. He decided to try his luck. To reach it took him two days. When he got there, he was met by a hostile farmer who set vicious dogs on him. He sustained a bad bite on the calf of his left leg.

His knowledge of traditional medicine came in handy. He treated himself with leaves and roots that had medicinal values.

Then he saw another big house, but to reach it, he

had to cross a big river. He had no problem because he could swim, but he did not know that there were crocodiles in the river. Taking off his skin clothes, he plunged into the water and there Mr Crocodile was waiting for him. The crocodile grabbed his foot and Tsepo struggled to free himself. Then suddenly a brilliant thought came to his mind. He threw his skin up so the crocodile thought it was him. It leaped up and Tsepo's foot was freed. He swam for the shore to save his life. His foot was bleeding and very painful. That night, he managed to climb on a tree and slept there. He feared wild animals would track him down because of the smell of blood from his wound.

The next day, he continued his search. He was very tired and hungry. He saw another house, and limped all the way to the gate. A tall thin man greeted him, but before he could talk, he collapsed. This man took him to one of the rondavels and when he came round, the man demanded to know who he was and what he wanted.

Tsepo told him his story. He was given food and a place to sleep. After a couple of days, his injuries were healed enough to start a job of herding cattle. He did not like this job, so after three years he left for the mines. He was employed as a cleaner and a gardener at the mine office. He often thought of his family in Lesotho. One day, he set out to visit them.

Although Tsepo had enough money for transport, there were no roads except the rocky footpaths on the hills, so he had to travel by foot. When finally he reached home, the people at home did not welcome him. He was no longer like them in many ways. He wore western clothes and had shoes on his feet. His sister looked at him and wondered how he got his feet into this moulded skin.

Tsepo did not stay long since the atmosphere was sour. He gave his father some money. His father had never seen money before and he did not know what to do with it. Tsepo was most welcomed by the mine people. They liked him because he was their traditional healer. He treated their minor ailments. Years passed, then it was time for Tsepo to retire. He became an old man who was lonely because he never married and was estranged from his family.

# The Thief

By Barbara Gumede

People were busy in and out of shops and even on the street they looked like ants collecting their food and storing it in the hole. It was the last Saturday of the month. People from all walks of life came to buy various items they needed and even the gangsters were there to do their mischief.

Don and his wife, Gladys, and their daughters, Grace and Mercy, were carrying groceries to the car. Don was pushing his way through the crowd. "I told you it was not advisable to shop at the end of the month," he said.

His wife replied, "It is cheaper during month-end. There are specials and price reductions on most articles."

"Come, girls, help me put these groceries in the boot so we can quickly get out of this place."

Suddenly, they heard people shout, "Catch the thief!" A young man of about twenty years ran past them carrying a big brown box. Police were running behind him. Just then a gunshot was heard and people ran for cover. Don and his family ducked down.

The young man was followed by police through the crowd. He crossed the road and disappeared in the passage and he was not carrying the brown box anymore. "I wonder what happened to the box?" Don asked himself. He continued loading his goodies into the boot when suddenly he saw the box inside the boot. He was shocked and closed the boot quickly. The police caught up with the thief and he was handcuffed as they came toward Don's car.

Don was shivering with fright. He did not know whether to reveal the box to the police or keep quiet and pretend he knew nothing. His heart was pounding fast as he started his car and drove off. "What is the matter, Don?" his wife asked.

"There is nothing wrong," replied Don.

Don was a chartered accountant and his wife, a senior lecturer. They lived in upper market of Drakefield where most doctors, magistrates, politicians and lawyers lived.

Don drove his German sedan into the double garage and ordered the girls to go inside the house, as he wanted to be alone with their mother.

"What is happening?" his wife asked.

Don opened the boot of the car where the brown box was. Written on the box was video cassette recorder. "How did it get here?" she asked.

"I do not know," replied Don. "You saw the young man who was chased by police? I think he is the one who threw it into the boot of our car."

"You should have told the police. This is stolen property!"

"I did think of doing that but I was afraid of what would happen to that young man. I think I know why he stole. Obviously, he was going to sell it and use the money to buy food for his family."

"I do not care about what you think of him. He is fit for jail!" snapped Gladys.

"If you had seen his eyes like I did, you would pity him," replied Don. Gladys said that she wanted the box to be taken to the police and if Don did not do it, she would report the matter to the police the next day.

On Sunday, Gladys and her two daughters went to church leaving Don alone at home.

There was a knock at the door and Don went to open it. Two young men came in. One had a scar across his forehead. Don quickly greeted them and went to the garage and came back with the brown box and handed it over to them, warning them never to say a word.

"I don't know you and you don't know me." With these words they went away.

Don decided to take his family for an outing. One

thing worried him though. How had those young men known where he lived? He decided to forget about the whole thing and enjoy himself with his family, returning home late in the evening.

The girls got out of the car first and ran to the house. They shouted very loudly, "DAD! MOM! HURRY!" Don and Gladys ran to the house only to find it was empty.

Everything had been stolen.

# Men and Mourning

By Phasekile Radebe

Are men exempted from mourning? It is normal that after the death of a family member, the whole family undergoes traumatic stress. They cry and express words of loss, they lose interest in many social things. They solemnly do everything quietly, speak softly, sing hymns in low tones, and actually go into depression. Surprisingly enough it is mostly women who undergo this phase.

If a woman loses her child, she sits on the mattress or mat until the funeral day, even if it takes a week or more before the burial of the deceased. She is repeatedly reminded to keep to the tradition. She is not even allowed to sleep on her bed, but on the floor mat.

When neighbours and relatives visit the bereaved family, they are directed to the lady on the mat, to be the "shock-absorber". Even the father of the deceased directs all visitors to her.

Is it not supposed to be a joint effort to share the pain and stress of losing a loved one? Men's behaviour does not seem to be affected nor altered. Are they exempted from the norms and traditions of our black people, or are they pretending to be more courageous?

In many instances, they hardly shed a tear. Is this a belief that men are not supposed to cry? But Jesus cried at the death of his friend Lazarus, and yes, he was a man too. Worse still, when the husband dies, even if he had been ill, the wife will be suspected of having killed him, or played a part in his death.

This suspicion is worse if it is a sudden death. An accusation usually comes from the relatives-in-law. They even ignore how much in love the couple had been.

The poor wife is expected to sit down covered with a rug, even on a hot summer day. She is not allowed even to stretch her legs and go to make tea in her own kitchen. She is only allowed up to eliminate.

If for any reason she is to do funeral arrangements, she must go wrapped up in a rug, and be a sight for sympathy from the public. If her tears run dry, then she is considered not to be worried about the death of her husband.

Come funeral day, everybody will observe how much crying she displays. Are tears still a tradition or a sign of emotion? If they are dry, where is she expected to get them from? Does this mean she is not hurting?

After the funeral, she commences her mourning period for a whole year, wearing black attire from head to toe. If she chooses to mourn in any other colour, such as navy or purple, she is considered not serious about the tradition. Worse, if she decides to not wear any symbolic attire, for some reasons, then she is considered to be happy about her husband being deceased.

Men are not confined to any specific mourning colour at the death of their wives.

In-laws and community members closely watch how she speaks to men. She is expected not to wear a smile for any man, let alone walk with one. No one even remembers that you had male relatives and family friends when your husband was still alive.

It is pathetic that some churches expect the mourning lady to sit right at the back of the church, and not mix freely with other members of the parish. Is that still an African Culture? And don't speak of any social get-togethers. It is taboo until she removes her mourning attire after twelve full months, and has been cleansed. Before that, she is not even expected to go through a head of cattle because of the belief that they will all die.

After the cleansing period, a cleansing ceremony is done. The lady's mourning attire is burned, or given to a very old lady (within the family circle). She goes to wash out of the house and then wears new clothes. Her marriage family slaughters a goat on different days to finalise her mourning period.

There is a vast difference between the handling of a bereaved female and that of a male. One wonders why because wedding vows are the same. Not much traditional rules are laid for a man who has lost his wife. He continues with his normal activities until the funeral day.

At the funeral service, the minister does not forget to comment that the man can get a replacement for his wife within a couple of months. The man hardly sheds a tear, yet his friends don't forget to give him what they call "after-tears" alcoholic drinks immediately they return from the ceremony.

He wears no mourning clothes. Nobody is worried about his behavioural patterns. Within one month, he satisfies his sexual needs, and that is considered to be normal. Within six months, he gets married, and the very minister who buried his wife guides him on his vows with his new wife, and life goes on for him, and the deceased is past history.

Were mourning cultural traditions meant for feminine gender only?

Why are men exempted from this very stressful customary behaviour?

# Do I Know My African Cultures, Norms and Values?

By Phasekile Radebe

*Grandchild:* Tell me a story that you like best.

*Granny:* There are so many of them, so you better tell me what you want to know.

*Grandchild:* Tell me how you came to marry Grandpa?

*Granny:* I was twenty-one years old before I fell in love. My father made me a feast noting that I was mature enough to have a boy friend. He slaughtered a cow, my mother brewed African beer, and I invited my friends for the celebration of my maturity.

My elder sisters thereafter taught me how to behave when I fell in love. They taught me that virginity was very important in the culture of an African girl. There were so many rules that I was supposed to know, and keep to the standards. I was not supposed to have sex. A man of my choice was to be approved by my elder sisters, and my parents. My man, or his parents were supposed to have cattle for payment of *labola* and other requirements.

*Grandchild:* Granny, was Grandpa a man of your choice, or a choice of your parents?

*Granny:* He was a man of my choice, but he was interviewed, to see if he met the required standards of a suitable husband to be. Even after passing his interview, we were not allowed to go out together until I was aware of safety precautions, to avoid pre-marriage pregnancy, as it was a taboo. Maintaining virginity until marriage was an honour to the girl, to her family, and to her community at large.

*Grandchild:* Granny, were you a virgin when you got married to Grandpa?

*Granny*: Yes, I was. Experienced women did constant examinations for maintenance of virginity to all unmarried girls of the area.

By virtue of my virginity, your Grandpa was ordered to pay an extra cow, additional to the ten *labola* cattle. That cow was called 'My Mother's Pride', and it symbolised a good family's education on culture, norms and values.

*Grandchild:* Granny, are my parents going to do the same examinations, and also choose a man for me? I don't think that I would agree to that. I want to make my own choice of my man, irrespective of whether he is rich or not.

*Granny*: They may not choose a boyfriend for you, but I do know that they would like you to abstain from sex before marriage, especially now that there is this killing incurable disease called HIV/AIDS, which you can get through sex. You know that your parents love you very much, and they would be miserable if you die, don't you? I also don't want to lose you through death, my dear Grandchild.

*Grandchild*: Granny, is my boyfriend not going to reject me and go to other girls if I refuse to have sex with him?

*Granny*: If he threatens to reject you, that will be when you know that he did not love you from the very word go. He just wanted you for a tool for his sex satisfaction. Forget about him, he is not your man. Your real man will respect you and your wishes.

*Grandchild*: Thank you, Granny. Always remember that I don't want to lose you either.

# You Are Now A Man, My Son

By Barbara Gumede

When I was a boy, I longed to be a man. To be recognised as a man in Xhosa custom, you had to be circumcised on the mountain. I asked my parents to allow me to go to the initiation school to be circumcised. They agreed.

It was the second of November when I left home. I could not help being afraid because of the terrible things that happen there. Some die of infection and never come home. I trusted our traditional practitioner. He was known for his good results.

My friends asked me repeatedly if I was serious about going to the mountain. I said, "Yes. I am serious because I want to be a man."

When I left home for Koffiestad, I knew there was no turning back. I paid my one hundred and forty rand, which was required to cover the procedure's expenses. A doctor's certificate was also required to certify that there was no infection. Some of the boys did not have these requirements and were sent home.

We were then advised to change our clothes and wrap ourselves in white blankets. To drink water was not allowed because your wound would not heal as expected. The *Inqcibi* (traditional doctor) did the procedure in the cattle kraal accompanied by three men. One of them was my uncle. It was a secret procedure.

It took only minutes before one was circumcised. I will never forget that moment for it changed my life. The pain was not as severe as some boys said. Life at the initiation school was not for the weak and feeble.

Western medicine was not allowed, only that which was given by the *Inqcibi* was allowed. There were no painkillers. You had to bear the pain and prove that you were a man. For some, the pain was so severe and unbearable that they ran away from the school to seek some help from clinics or hospitals.

Those who ran away were never considered to be men. They are boys, for they had shown weakness and cowardice.

It was pathetic, because when they go back home after having failed to cope with the pain and having taken treatments other than those provided at the initiation school, they were segregated from those who had successfully completed the requirements.

When the school was over, the rest of the boys returned home to their parents.

The whole village rejoiced and prepared a big feast in their honour. Beasts were slaughtered and beer flowed. The elders of the kraal had given me lessons on how to behave.

It is dangerous to go to these initiation schools run by unqualified men. They have ruined many young boys' lives. Infection is the main cause of death. My father was extremely proud of me.

He told me, "You are now a man, my son."

# Ukwemula

By Gloria Gladys Khanyile

*Ukwemula* is the equivalent to the celebration of the twenty-first birthday of a girl in African culture. Below is a description of this ceremony in Zulu culture.

As people were illiterate and did not know the ages in years, they used the physical appearance and maturity of the young woman to gauge her age.

The girls were divided into groups according to their age. When the girl reached puberty, she would be called a "*jongosi*" and was regarded as young, only considered to be at an early milestone of womanhood.

As she ages in the following years, rounding at the hips, gaining weight etc – approximately at eighteen years of age, she progresses from a "*jongosi*" to a "*tshitshi*". At this stage, the parents would slaughter a goat or two for her in celebration. This ceremony is called "*umhlonyane*".

Then, after this, comes the celebration called '*ukwemula*' that the girl celebrates in her early twenties, approximately at twenty-one years of age.

Nowadays, particularly in the locations and urban areas, this celebration is carried out at the celebration of the 21st birthday, and is ideally celebrated over a weekend.

When the day of celebration has been stipulated, three days prior to the day, the girl hides herself from people "*Ukugoya*". Only her female peers keep her company there.

In the rural areas she stays in her kraal *(ilawu)* and only her peers are allowed in. During this seclusion period, she covers her head and face completely so that she is not seen. In the late afternoon, she, together with her peers, go out to their neighbours and move from house to house singing. The people understand what this is all about and they shower her with gifts. This act of going around is called "*Ukuzoyisa*" and no letter of invitation is written to people, as this is a way of inviting them to the ceremony.

On the eve of the ceremony, the girl goes to her maternal family to fetch a spear. She uses this spear on the day of the ceremony, as it will be explained later. When she gets to the maternal family, they already know she is coming and have the spear ready. She arrives with her peers singing with her. She has to look for the spear, because they hide it and she has to find it herself.

When she finds it, there is jubilation and celebration in the house and they are entertained. In the midst of the celebration, the entourage leaves the maternal family home in a hurry without saying any goodbyes. She takes her spear along with her. (She goes to the maternal family only if she is still single and unattached; if she is already engaged, she has to collect the spear at her fiancés home.)

On the day of the ceremony, the girl, with her entourage, should have spent the previous night under a tree in rural areas, but in the location she uses the same room of seclusion or a neighbour offers her a place. At this place, they wash themselves, dress up and make up there before moving to her house for the ceremony. (In rural areas, after spending the night under the tree, they go down to the river and wash, dress up and make up there).

On arrival at home, her father points the spot just outside the home where the whole dancing and singing will take place. This spot remains a secret until the entourage comes and only then are they shown where it will be. This is kept a secret so that people do not bewitch the spot, keeping the girls from falling ill or even dying.

At home, her father slaughters a cow. Men cook the meat whilst women cook various traditional, as well as modern dishes, because at the end of the dancing ceremony, everybody will enjoy lunch.

The girl dresses up in a skin skirt and a traditional headgear (*isicholo*). Over her shoulders and chest she wears the peritoneum (*umhlwehlwe* or the membrane from the slaughtered cow's abdomen). The girl closest to the one who is celebrating, wears the same attire as her, except for the peritoneum. She is called "*impelesi*" meaning she is accompanying her.

On the day of the ceremony, the girl's entourage is joined by young men, who will all dance and sing.

At the start of the ceremony, the maternal family are the first to come forward. They come with gifts, particularly those of blankets, and they pin money onto her headgear. The next to come are her family, who also give her gifts and pin money on her head gear, then comes the rest of the crowd, neighbours, relatives, and friends from far and wide. Not all the people come to her spontaneously. Instead, she has to go to them. She goes with her spear, given by the maternal family, and picks on any person by thrusting the spear on the ground in front of that person and moves back to the dancing spot, leaving the spear behind. The closest person takes the spear back to her, utters some praises to her, or simply performs a dance in front of her, and then pins money on her headgear. The girl moves out again with the spear to pick another person. This goes on for a long time, until all people who intend giving her gifts have come forward. There is a lot of entertainment, excitement and ululating during these performances.

The young men and girls perform dances in groups and as individuals. The celebrant herself joins in the dancing groups as well as dance alone then she moves out again with her spear as before. By this time, her headgear looks like a Christmas tree with hanging notes of R200, R100, R50, R20 and R10s depending on her popularity. At the end of the ceremony, there is so much money on her headgear that there is hardly any space left for pinning more notes. Over and above this money, there are a lot of gifts she gets from friends and family.

When she has exhausted the crowds, she together with her girl entourage, leaves the ceremony spot in a hurry. They actually run away home. They quickly change their attire when they leave. The whole crowd follows them home where a big party starts. The celebrant and her entourage help in serving people with food and meat.

The money she obtains from the ceremony is usually banked and together with some of the gifts she obtains from the ceremony, helps her in preparation for her marriage in the near future.

# The Process of a Zulu marriage

By Victoria Ngane Cele

## Stage I

### Engagement (*lobolo*)

In Zulu culture, marriage is taken so seriously that it cannot just happen overnight. There are steps that are followed and requirements to be met by the two parties. Those steps and requirements are so important that if omitted, it is believed that the marriage will not work, will not succeed, will not prosper and may not even give fruit i.e. the bearing of children. This needs commitment and understanding, and therefore the preparations deeply involve the parents, the elders, God and the Ancestors.

This custom is carried out with great respect and honour, because it is a means of creating good relationships between the families in question. It starts with two people, who have been in love and courting for a number of years and have come to a decision to start their own family. This decision in Zulu culture comes from the male partner who proposes to the female partner. He then informs his parents. He must have worked for years saving money to make sure that when he starts the procedure of going to his girlfriends parents, he has enough cattle required as "*Lobolo*".

Having satisfied himself of his savings, he breaks the news to his eldest brother, who passes it on to his father. The father then calls the young man to confirm what he has been informed by the eldest son. After confirming, a special meeting of the family members is called. The members include uncles, elders and all males who are prominent in this family.

At this meeting, the young man will then show the family members the cash he has accumulated over the years and the number of cattle he owns in his father's cattle kraal, and if not enough, some additional cattle could be offered by his father to assist him. The meeting will be briefed about the girl's family - status, and situation, and a date for sending delegates to represent the family is set.

In the mean time, the young man proposes again to his girlfriend and asks her to pass the news to her family.

One such young man is Sifiso, who is on holiday from Johannesburg. His young lady is Thulisile, who stays with her parents in the village. She helps do the housework at home.

One afternoon they meet at their usual secluded spot.

Sifiso says, "Thulie, my darling, I feel we have been in love for long enough, that we understand each other and we are both grown up enough to be able to start a family of our own. My mother and father would love to see our children while still alive, and more so, my mother is an old lady, who needs a younger daughter to assist her at home. We have discussed this with her and my sisters and everyone's choice was you, my Thulie. The ball is then yours, my dear. Will you marry me and be part of the Ndosie family?"

After a big pause of silence and showing great respect and appreciation of what has been said to her, she smiles and replies, "My Ndosie, it has always been my wish, since I fell in love with you, to spend the rest of my life with you, till death do us part, but remember starting a family is not child's play. I hope you mean what you say."

Sifiso replied, "This is not a joke, my dear. To prove my honesty, I will ask you to inform your family that at the end of the month, my father will send delegates to your family, to ask for good human relationship."

Thulisile hugs Sifiso affectionately. They kiss each other and depart saying bye-bye.

Thulisile quietly visits her grandma's hut after supper, saying, "Good evening, Grandma, how are you? I have been missing you a lot."

Her Grandma replied, "Oh yes, my grand daughter, I have been missing you too. Are you still behaving well with that boyfriend of yours?"

Thulisile smiled. "Yes, well, grandmother (*gogo*)," she answers giggling as this question tickles her very much.

Grandma says, "I am pleased to hear that. You know, Thulie, you must always remember that I am proud of you. I am looking forward to you having a white wedding, and trust that you keep your virginity till that day; so do not disappoint us – your father and the whole family."

"I promise, Grandma, that it will be so. Today's visit is special. It has good news about your friend – Ndosie boy, as you call him."

Grandma smiled. "Hey, come sit next to me so that I can hear this interesting news, I cannot wait to hear it, more so, since you know my ears cannot hear well."

Thulisile sat next to her Grandma, and said, "Granny, Sifiso says he loves me so much that he proposed to marry me. He would like to be with me for the rest of his life."

Grandma smiled broadly. "That is very good news to hear. Remember I told you that Ndosie boy looks an honest, loving young man and he comes from a well-to-do family."

"Oh yes, Grandma, he has been very faithful to me over the years. He has spoken to his parents and they intend coming here at the end of this month, when Sifiso is on holiday," said Thulisile.

"Alright then, I'll have to let your mother know about this and you have to let your eldest sister know, so that she informs all the girls in the village. Your mother, your sisters and myself will start preparing quietly the Zulu beer."

## Stage II

### Visit to the in-laws-to-be

At the beginning of the week (Tuesday), preparations of brewing Zulu Beer are commenced at the homes of both families. This is started early in the week, being the proper customary trend. Zulu Beer must take days to brew so that the Ancestors can feel and inhale the smell, and be told of what is going to take place in these homes.

It is always very important for each household, before starting preparations for any event, to inform God (*Mvelinqangi*) and the Ancestors. A holy sanctified liquid or mixture called an *'intelezi"* is sprinkled all over the household's yards and gardens. The person who does this is the father. As he moves around the yard, he talks to the Ancestors, sprinkling at the same time, and asking for peace and happiness, patience and understanding between each other during the talks by the two families. All the time he says praises of the family.

In the morning of the departure of delegates, everybody wakes up early. Special prayers are said, asking God and the Ancestors to accompany them, to guide them in their journey, and, as they talk to their equals, to be brave.

On their arrival, the delegates stand about fifteen metres away from the household. The older delegate speaks aloud, saying praises of that household. By so doing, he introduces the visiting family, who they are, where they are from, and the purpose of their visit.

The reader must remember that the people of the girl's home are indoors. Maybe it is in winter and it may take some time to attend to the delegate's calls. Sometimes, the delayed attention is done deliberately to test the delegates. If they mean what they say, they will have to persevere. The call of praises may even last for thirty minutes before being responded to.

DELEGATE: - "Hail! Bayede nina bakewa Keswa Nozuko! We humbly request your mercy and acceptance from your household to relate to you the message that comes from our elders – KwaCele, Ndosie, Khumlbuza, Nkomo isengwa ilele, to earnestly request for Good Human Relationship between these two families. We have been attracted by a 'beautiful Rose' within your family.

"We are presenting eleven cattle, all livestock. The first one is for her mother, Umqhoyiso." This cow is very significant because it proves the virginity of the young girl. If the girl is no longer a virgin or has a child, this cow is omitted.

Then they continue. The ten following cattle are for the father called "Annabheka", so called because he has been her guardian. They are, he says, five black and white and five brown and white.

Before being let into the gates, there is a fee that must be paid by the delegates. They stand at the gate until they are told to pay because if they do not, they are not allowed to enter. The first fee is called *"Imvulamasango"*, meaning, "permission to enter the household".

All elders - males only - may attend this meeting. The main speaker from the delegates will break the news directly to the father of the household and elders. He repeats all what he has been shouting at the gate in the same systematic manner. The father may not respond purposely and may not say a word until someone from the family members gives them a tip advising that the father needs a Mouth opener (*Imvulamlomo*) or tooth opener (*Ingqaqamazinyo*) so as to be able to respond to them and suggests that a fee of about ten rand at least, be paid immediately, because if not paid, there will be no progress.

When this amount of money has been paid, the young lady's father starts talking to the delegates. He greets them, welcomes them to his Ancestors and father's household and asks them again the purpose for their visit, and what they have with them in the line of Lobolo. The delegate would answer with great respect, and repeat correctly what he had said before. At this stage, the lady in question will be called, for her to be asked if she knows the delegates or not, because if she has no knowledge of them, the elders cannot accept them, and they would be turned back.

Two other girls should accompany her, one of whom will be her spokesperson and will answer all questions on her behalf.

The three ladies enter the room in a respectful manner; faces cast downwards in a very humble manner, and sit on a floor mat provided for this purpose.

The father would ask the delegates which one of these ladies was the lady in question, that is, the future daughter-in-law. The delegate would then have to answer correctly because he must already know which of the three ladies is their future daughter-in-law.

The father would then turn to the three girls, using his bold fatherly voice, "Thulie, do you know these people?"

The spokes lady replies, "Yes, Daddy, we know them."

The father then dismisses the girls. "Alright, girls, you may now leave."

The girls leave the room appearing very shy.

After making sure that the girls have left, the discussions continue.

The father tells the delegate, "Now you can continue with your request."

And the delegate says, "I repeat your highness, that a young man from the Cele family was attracted by your Rose, and because these two love each other, the Cele family has sent us to ask for a Good Human Relationship between the two families."

The father then says, "Now you can tell me what you have to offer."

The delegate responds, "We have eleven cattle to offer. Firstly, one black and white jersey cow for our mother-in-law. The next ten are for the father-in-law, five being black and white oxen, and the other five being brown and white cows."

The mother-in-law's cow should be paid on this very day. This is the 'virginity cow', that the mother and the whole family are proud of. The young lady has preserved her virginity.

The last, but not least, would concern the old ladies (grannies) not only from this home, but also from neighbours. They are called to come and get their sweets, and snuff tobacco from the son-in-law.

They are accepted, the now friendly parties talk to each other on different issues, while one or two goats are slaughtered. Food and beer are then served and everybody is happy.

Before departure, the delegates are given a list of items that will be gifts for the mother, father and other prominent members of the family.

The bringing over of these gifts is a separate occasion (mini wedding) in which all the prominent members from the bride's family will gather to receive their presents from their new son-in-law. On this day, the bride-to-be will also be dressed from top to bottom by her in-laws in an outfit they feel is suitable for their new daughter-in-law. A date for this occasion will be selected on this day.

## Stage III

### Bringing Over Of The *Lobola* Cattle

This is a very big event because even the neighbours are invited to see the cattle.

The preparations are done as usual, early in the week, the brewing of Zulu beers, spring-cleaning, the collecting of wood, and groceries. Neighbours and relatives donate some groceries. Reporting to God and the Ancestors is done, and this is a custom, whenever there are crowds of people gathering in any African household. God and Ancestors are informed so as to be warned and make peace during the event.

On the day, at the groom-to-be's home, the same preparations happen, prayers asking God and the Ancestors to guide and protect them as they go and deliver.

When they arrive at their destination, they will call, as they did before. This time, everybody at this place is awake waiting. The cattle kraal (*isibaya*) is opened for the cattle to enter.

The delegate says, "Here are your cattle, your highness," saying family praises such as, "Nazuko – the colours are so and so," until he finishes them all. At this time, everybody is very happy, singing praises, congratulations, and the women are ululating. The cattle are led into their kraal (*esibayeni*).

On this day, the bride's party will have also prepared some welcoming preparations for the groom's family in the line of beasts slaughtered.

One goat for the groom, to eat at his in-laws. One goat for his mother, also to eat. Another goat will be for the eldest sister-in-law (*inkosazana*), also for her to eat at this place. The last goat will be for the main delegate (*umkhongi*). All these goats are known as *indlakudla* – 'permission to eat at this home'.

As regards the *Lobolo*, the number of cattle offered

to the girl's family is not always the same, just as the status of people also is not always the same.

For a girl born of a commoner, it is eleven, and for a girl born of an *Induna/Counsellor* it is sixteen cattle. A girl born of a Chief/Royal Family, the *lobolo* is twenty-five to thirty cattle.

When a Chief takes his wives, only one of those wives will be for the Nation. Therefore, everybody in the community will be expected to contribute at least one beast or cow for that purpose. The first baby son born will be the heir to the throne.

## Stage IV

### The Bringing of Gifts (*Izibizo*)

A few months later, after the engagement that is, *Lobolo*, the groom's party returns to the bride-to-be's household to present the gifts that were requested by the womenfolk on the engagement day.

The gifts would be for the prominent members of the family, namely, father, mother, grandparents, aunts, sisters and brothers. The bride's mother gets more gifts, for instance, a big blanket of good quality, and a smaller one for her waist, a pinafore, head-*doek,* a twenty-five litre three-legged pot, 12.5kg of sugar, 12.5kg of cake flour, teabags, bulk lantern paraffin, washing basin, soap and towel, baby vaseline and baby powder and so on.

All the above items are an indication that the bride-to-be was once a baby. Her mother had to wake up at night, light the lantern or candles when feeding, or changing her napkin, the washing basin and the rest were to show that she was bathed when she was a baby. If there are aunts and sisters in the family, each would be presented with an apron and a head-*doek,* brothers would be presented with a shirt and tie each. The younger brother would get a suit or a bicycle depending on what he had wanted. Then, lastly, but not least, their bride-to-be would be dressed from head to toe in a beautiful dignified outfit, that is, a hat, costume, stockings, shoes and a handbag.

This outfit is called *isidwaba* or hide-skirt by which she is accepted as their daughter-in-law and also shows her how she is expected to dress up in a beautiful, dignified, respectable manner – dressing up like a married woman and not a teenager.

The father-in-law may ask for an overcoat, a hat and a walking stick. In older days when horses were a means of transport, he would request a fully saddled horse, and this would be offered to him.

On the day of presentation, the usual preparations and procedures that were done before departure, occur. On the other side, preparations for welcoming visitors also occur.

In some places, among these visitors is the groom's mother, who comes to witness the dressing up of her daughter-in-law. When these visitors arrive at the gate, they sing songs, which indicate that they are bringing gifts to the household. The bride's party come out of the household, also singing to meet their visitors. They bring refreshments. They also bring a mat to sit on, a blanket for the mother-in-law to put over her shoulders, basin, soap and towel and a head-*doek*. She would then be asked to sit on the mat with her sister, her shoulders covered with the small blanket, the head-*doek* tied around her head and given the basin, towel and soap to take home – this is a custom to show her welcome and respect.

After having some refreshments, the female visitors and groom's party would form a procession. Each female carries on her head a parcel containing a gift, and follows each other, singing. The wife of the main delegate (*umka Mkhongi*) carries the lid of the three-legged pot, and leads the procession, the heavy pot is carried by males. When they arrive at the area prepared for them, the parcels are put down. The wife of the Main delegate would remain standing with the lid of the big pot on her head.

The groom's party offers her money demanded by the lid carrier. She is then helped to take the lid off her head. All the time people are happy, women carrying brooms and green leaves, ululating, and there is great joy at this household.

When everybody is seated and comfortable, all the members of the family would join the groom's party. A prayer is said and the Ancestors are informed of what is happening. The father of the bride-to-be gives a welcoming speech, so that everybody feels at home. All the people presented are seated in an orderly manner, waiting to be called.

The groom's sister does the presentations. A floor mat is laid on the floor so that each member sits while being presented. She would start with the father, with great respect; she would call upon the father of the household (*ubaba wekhaya*). Customarily, the first things put in front of him are a beer pot (*ukhamba*) that is placed on a decorated grass mat (*isithebe*) and the pot covered with a decorated grass cover (*imbenge*).

The mother would then follow. She is offered her gifts and everyone else follows. The most interesting part in this procedure is that each and every person, after receiving his or her gifts, shows gratitude by doing some traditional dance, singing his or her favourite song for dancing. The rest of the people clap hands, sing along and start ululating. The last, but not least, will be the bride-to-be. The groom's sister goes with few young ladies into a room that is prepared for them to dress her up. When they are finished, they come out singing proudly that the bride is theirs, no matter what. At this juncture, the bridegroom joins them.

When they reach the stage or area where the spectators are, the bride-to-be, beautifully dressed, would move around a little, modelling, just to show how her outfit fits her. There is more joy and ululating as she moves. There is traditional dancing with both parties competing. Food and drinks are then served.

It is the Zulu Custom that when food is served, people are categorised according to their age groups. The groom's party gets special attention (V.I.P.). They are served in a special room, or area prepared for them, as a sign of respect.

When it is time for departures, the families gather and say a prayer, the father of the household leads, gives thanks, and wishes his visitors and guests a safe journey home.

## Stage V

### Demonstration of Gratitude – *Umbondo-Ingqibamasondo*

This occasion is a symbol whereby the bride-to-be shows gratitude to her in-laws for the cattle and the gifts received by her parents.
It is called *Ngqibamasondo* because:
- GQIBA means 'to cover', and,
- MASONDO means 'the hooves of the cattle'.

She then offers edible gifts also, in return, to show gratitude to them for recognizing her and highlighting her place in the community.

All the young ladies and young men are invited. A date is set on which they should go to the groom's place with these edible gifts. It is customary that on this day, a goat will be slaughtered, allowing her to eat at the in-law's. Among these edibles are bags of potatoes, oranges, pumpkin, sweet potatoes, beans, rice, mealie meal, flour, sugar, and tea. There will also be a special basket for the groom's mother which contains all sorts of nice things like sausages, soups, sweets, and chocolates. The bride will herself carry this basket on her head and present it to her mother in-law. There is a lot of joy and ululating, singing, and everyone is very happy.

There will then be a short meeting of the families, setting the wedding date, after which the father of the household gives thanks and wishes them a safe journey.

## Stage VI

### Kitchen Party – *Ukucimela*

A few months before the wedding, the bride-to-be visits her relatives, going from house to house. If they are far, she even spends a night with them to bid them good-bye, as she would soon be going to stay with her in-laws for the rest of her life. Another reason for visiting her relatives is to ask for presents, which usually include floor mats, brooms, clay pots and wooden spoons. These presents would be useful at her new home. This custom got the name '*Cimela*' meaning 'closing eyes', because when she arrives at her relatives house, she will simply close her eyes and not say a word. Looking at her, people will know what she has come for, and will give her any of the household items mentioned above, and she will thank them, and jokes and laughter would follow, and she then continues on her journey to other relatives. This, nowadays, is known as a "kitchen party."

Besides gifts from relatives, other people, neighbours and friends, as soon as they are told that so and so is about to get married, they all help make what we now call 'trousseau' or 'bottom drawer' for her free of charge. This may consist of floor mats, tablemats, wooden spoons, and brooms to equip her for her house.

## Stage VII

## The Wedding

After wedding preparations are made and invitations are sent all over the village, the bride-to-be is kept in isolation for a month, with her maids. The bride's father slaughters a goat and a cow to bid his daughter farewell. He informs his Ancestors, asking them to accompany the girl, guide her, and keep her safe wherever she goes. He then removes the bile from the slaughtered cow, and pours it over the girl's head, face and all the joints of her arms and feet (upper and lower limbs). This custom is known as '*ukucola*'.

The old ladies gather in the kraal where the bride-to-be is isolated. They examine her, and do a Virginity test. Qualified experts, who check for the existence of the hymen, do this. They also counsel her thoroughly, giving her good advice on how to run a home, and how to behave, and treat her in-laws, no matter how difficult circumstances may be. She is told to expect the good and the bad, but she must be brave and have respect. She is told that she must not spoil the good name of her parents. They will also give her blessings, pray to God and her Ancestors for her, for a good, safe, and long life.

After pouring or anointing her with bile, the father takes his daughter by hand out of the kraal, walks around, reporting to the Ancestors that the girl is now leaving for the new home. (In Zulu custom, the cattle kraal resembles a temple).

On the day of departure, many people accompany the bride. They walk the distance and the bride does not look back, so that even if things became tough, she would not think of going back home.

When they arrive at the gates of in-laws, they are offered meat from a goat that had been specially slaughtered for their welcome. This is known as 'Removal of a barrier' *(ukususa umgoqo)*.

At the groom's place, special rooms are prepared for the bride's party to occupy. Immediately, the groom's party, consisting of young men and ladies, come and join in. They stay the whole night, talking, joking, singing and having fun. The mixing of grooms' and brides' parties for the whole night is called *Ukugqunyushelwa* (socialising). At the groom's place, a cow is slaughtered for the bride's party, but the bride does not eat the meat from it. She uses the meat that was her provision from home. On the wedding day, the bride's party go to the river very early to bath. On their return, the bride wears a New Skin Skirt (*Isidwaba)* that has been carefully made, powdered and oiled with oils of best quality. Around her arms and legs, she wears white fluffy arm and leg bands. Her bust is covered with white beads. On her head, she wears a veil made of leaves from a special tree for this purpose. It is called '*Imvakaza*'. In her right hand, she carries a short sword or stick knife called '*Isinqindi*'.

All of the above shows that she is a virgin, and in Zulu custom, this confirms it to be a white wedding. The other girls of her age group also wear skin skirts and beads.

On the dancing floor, at the groom's home, there is dancing and singing. The two parties compete, taking turns. As they dance, women ululate and clap hands.

## Stage VIII

## Presentation of Gifts – *Umabo*

This is a very important Zulu custom of offering gifts and presents to the in-laws. The bride would not only present members of the immediate family but would also offer to the members of the extended families, that is, uncles, aunts and cousins. The last but not least, she would present her husband as well. When presented, each member shows gratitude by singing and dancing. This makes the wedding very exciting with clapping of hands and ululating.

When the presentation is over the bride's father hands over his daughter. This is called *'Ukuthethelela nokuyala'* –that is, bidding farewell and last counselling.

Firstly the father introduces her, saying who she is, born of which family, saying praises of his ancestors. He would also ask God and the Ancestors to bless his daughter at this new home and also to be blessed with children.

If his daughter had any sickness he would not hide that and if she has good health he would say so. He would also announce that the *lobolo* was paid in full.

The marriage counsellor (*Induna*) appointed by the chief then assists the couple to take their marriage vows. The bride would then sing her favourite song. She would dance with her maids. She does this very well because this is the last dance she does whilst still a maiden, proudly carrying her short sword.

Lastly, the groom's father would speak, thanking God and the Ancestors for the lovely daughter-in-law and also giving his blessings to the couple. The couple would then be accompanied to their well-prepared room. The bride's party would then leave for their home on the same day but one of the young maids remains with the bride so as to help her doing work and moving around as the bride may not move as she pleases. This lady is called an *Impelesi* or *Umhlalisi* or *Makotshana.* There are some areas that she is not allowed to go during this orientation period. For the next three months after the wedding, the newly-wed bride does not visit her maiden home. This is post wedding (quarantine) period for better orientation.

Lightning Source UK Ltd.
Milton Keynes UK
UKHW021837081121
393628UK00005B/165